Also by Kathleen Shoop

Historical Fiction:
The Donora Story Collection
After the Fog—Book One
The Strongman and the Mermaid—Book Two

The Letter Series
The Last Letter—Book One
The Road Home—Book Two
The Kitchen Mistress—Book Three
The Thief's Heart—Book Four
The River Jewel—A Letter Series Novella

Tiny Historical Stories
Melonhead—One
Johnstown—Two

Romance:
Endless Love Series:
Home Again—Book One
Return to Love—Book Two
Tending Her Heart—Book Three

Women's Fiction:
Love and Other Subjects

Bridal Shop Series
Puff of Silk—Book One

THE CHRISTMAS COAT

KATHLEEN SHOOP

shoop@kshoop.com

Kshoop.com

ISBN-13: 9781711321882

CHAPTER 1

The noise. Dear God, the voices. Teen boys—the shifting vocal tenors, the girls, squealing instead of simply talking. They wouldn't shut up and Elliot Ebberts couldn't hear his own thoughts. And it was nearly Christmas, dammit. The happiest time of the year, yet all he felt was tension tangling in his belly.

I wish I was at my meeting. I wish I didn't have to do all this crap.

He turned up the radio when he heard the opening strains of "Rudolph the Red-Nosed Reindeer." The kids joined in and Elliot soothed himself with the thought he was nearly finished with his unexpected, inconvenient drop-off duties. He puffed his cheeks, tapping the steering wheel, waiting for the crossing guard to move a barge-load of kids across traffic-jammed Hulton Road. Elliot's mind raced to where he should have already been—at the apartment building in East Liberty, doing the final walk-through before closing. Later, after dinner at Mulvaney's with Libby and the kids, he would give his wife the best Christmas present he could imagine.

A mitten brushed past Elliot's ear, whipped from the back of the SUV, landing on the dashboard. Silence descended on the vehicle before the teens in the back erupted with laughter. Elliot spun around, glaring. His son, Benji, in the passenger seat, dropped his face into his hands and hissed, "Dad, please."

"What?" Elliot's irritation matched their hilarity, but he swallowed it like a good father, like his wife had taught him to do after "it" happened. "It" was when he once roared like a wounded lion at a group of six-year-old boys. Their play had devolved from a nice game of backyard baseball to targeting each other with a barrage of leather gloves. Dodge ball with expensive, leather baseball gloves.

He'd never forget the look on his wife Libby's face, her disappointment. Her upset hadn't been aimed at the boys for being so careless with their new gloves. Instead she scolded him for overreacting. Her suggestion was for Elliot to teach them how to temper their natural boyish instinct to pelt each other with whatever was handy.

"Don't you see what you're doing?" she had spat at him as they entered the family room through the French doors, out of earshot of the boys. "You're acting just like your father."

Those words had stung. He didn't want that. And it wasn't true. Yet each of Libby's indictments had landed hot, branding him. And so from then on he'd tried every day—no, every minute—to never spew hot anger over a group of rowdy boys or screeching girls again.

Elliot grabbed the pink mitten with the knitted nubs. "Whose?" He held it up to the crew in the back two rows. Even his daughter, Clementine, was struggling not to laugh. Jeffery Jonas gave him that mocking teen smile that was inspired by nothing more than the sight of an adult attempting to be parental.

"Hey Jesus, Jeff," Elliot said. "Get your ass off my coat. That's a good coat. Really expensive and…"

"Dad," Benji said without actually looking at his father.

The tension in the car was thick as the fat mitten. Jeffery leaned forward and snatched it back. "Sorry 'bout that. It's for the clothing drive." Jeffery patted his chest. "Just trying to wrench open the old heart, let in the Christmas spirit, revel in the true meaning of the holiday season."

Elliot narrowed his eyes on Jeffery. "I'd bet dollars to donuts this is for your college essay."

"Mr. Ebberts, that's cynical."

"Then penance for driving your parents crazy."

Jeffery shrugged. "I know I'm your favorite, Mr. Ebberts. You can try to pretend your distaste for me runs deep…" Jeffery patted his chest again. "But I know you believe in the Christmas season more than any of us. I'm just trying to be generous and kind."

Smart-ass. "Oh, a future philanthropist in the carpool. How lucky for us."

"Future? I'm already fully engaged in philanthropy." He shifted the enormous garbage bag on his lap.

"So you're giving away your parents' clothing. Very charitable."

"Have to start somewhere, Mr. Ebberts. All things great and small…"

Elliot grimaced. He swallowed the rest of his comments. Later he would bring this up as Exhibit A to Libby as to why Benji was choosing his friends poorly. Mocking an adult with all this feigned generosity.

"Yep," Jeffery said. "Just airing out the old heart for the holidays."

"Umm hmm." It had to be for the essay. Jeffery hadn't cornered the market on smarts, so acts of charity might be his only avenue into a university next year.

Benji glared at his father, begging and warning him to disengage right that second.

Elliot didn't need to get himself more worked up. So he blew out his air. "Well, keep the mittens in the donation bag, then, Bill Gates, because your kind contribution won't do any good if you leave it behind in my car."

Elliot turned back to the road in front of him. Spurts of laughter broke through, reminding him of when he and his friends used to try to hold in laughter in class, their shoulders bobbing, faces beet red. He shook his head. It was like none of these kids took him seriously.

Horns blared and he realized he was holding up traffic. The crossing guard was wind-milling her arm, her face full of irritation that he hadn't been paying attention. Elliot eased into the next segment of the gauntlet—the drop-off line. Situated behind a woody station wagon that paused behind a Navigator that was behind a bus at the high school, they all waited.

The group of vehicles ahead of Elliot's released chattering kids onto the sidewalk. Granite-heavy packs bent them like reeds in the wind as they puffed cotton ball breaths into the cold air. A light snow dusted the pavement as holiday music blared from the bakery across the street, and car horns screamed from behind.

"Move up, Dad. You're only supposed to leave six inches between vehicles," Benji said.

"Seriously? Someone's measuring?"

Benji shrugged. Elliot inched his Mercedes SUV closer.

Another horn blare came. Elliot glanced in the rearview mirror, grinding his teeth to keep from shooting the finger at the impatient nutjob beeping behind him. Pete, the chubby second baseman from last season, was cutting an unsanctioned path across Third Street and Elliot chastised himself for not thinking of parking there to dump off the kids. *Genius.* He gave a nod to Pete's dad before the man sped into faster moving traffic.

Pete clipped the front corner of Elliot's car with his Santa-sized donation sack. He was followed by another kid whose arms were stacked high with wrapped parcels that blocked his view and made him feel his way with his toes, like a tightrope walker.

Elliot looked in his side mirror, wishing Libby hadn't had to work a double, pulling the night shift at the hospital. Any other day. He rapped his fingers on the steering wheel again then turned off the Christmas music. Body heat from the teens mashed into the back had steamed up the windows. Clementine's friend Maggie now traced her finger through the condensation.

Elliot wanted to tell her to stop, but Benji followed his gaze and elbowed his father. "Please. I'll clean it later."

Elliot watched Maggie finish her design—a heart with Jeffery's name in the center. *Jeffery?* He scoffed and shook his head. *Aim higher, dear girl.*

Benji visibly relaxed in the passenger seat when it became obvious his father was keeping this scolding to himself.

Elliot blew out another puff of held air. For two weeks, stress had caused him to move like a bear just out of hibernation, cranky, hungry, to be avoided, so he wanted to make it up to Libby. He wanted to do something meaningful, big for her this Christmas. No jewelry—she didn't like flashy things she had to take off before every nursing shift—so Elliot had come up with something monumental. He was purchasing a building just for her.

The large Victorian home had been divided into apartments. Libby had lived there until college, but now it was an inch from being condemned. Its purchase and the plan to tear it down and rebuild would be a breathtaking gift in every sense, something Libby would never forget. And she deserved that kind of present. This project would help revitalize the neighborhood she loved, plus it would be the perfect way to kick off the family's Christmas break.

Finally, it was time for the cars to move into the drop-off circle. Once at the curb, social media pressure wielded by parents like a hammer to the head, demanded the car be empty and moving again in half a minute.

Only ten seconds passed and the mother in the car behind him was already heavy on the horn. Carol Peabody? Or was it that whiny Amy McHaney shaking her fist at him? The glare from the snow melting on her windshield hid her identity.

"Roll up a little more, Dad," Benji said. "She can't get into the circle."

Elliot groaned and did as asked before throwing the SUV into park. "Everybody out! Your mother'll kill me if we end up on the Facebook drop-off naughty list thingy."

"Shit list, Mr. Ebbert. It's a shit list," said Spaulding, the only quiet kid in the car, who pushed the car door open and dragged out his backpack, a project storyboard and a bag full of canned goods for the food drive.

"No swearing, God dammit." Elliot said into his hand. The holidays brought out the worst in Elliot Ebberts.

Clementine reached around the seat and gave her father a peck, her lip gloss sticking to his cheek. "Chill, Dad. Your blood pressure'll spike and you'll turn tomato-red again. Then one of your secretaries will be on 911 and Mom'll freak. Again."

She hopped out of the car as he wiped his face, amazed at her calm. "See you at the restaurant. Wait 'til you see what I bought your mom for Christmas." He lowered his window and waved as she cut around the front of his car, smiling the way his wife used to when they first met, back when she was Elliot's biggest fan. "She's gonna love it."

"Can't wait, Dad," Clementine said. "See you then!"

The last of the kids barreled out of the car, dragging all manner of bags and projects. Elliot refused to turn back to see what a mess they had made. Today was too important to focus on nonsense. Shouldn't there be a carpool service for times like this? When important things had to be accomplished?

Shrieking horns disoriented Elliot and before he knew it, he'd shoved his hand through the window, middle finger up, fanning it slowly backward and forward. People waiting to turn into the circle mouthed angry words through closed windows. His head swiveling, every single person seemed to be pissed at him.

He gripped the wheel and edged around a minivan that was hemorrhaging kids. The mother in the van glowered, shaking her head at Elliot. He paused and put his window down. "Ha-ha! You're taking too long and I'm adding you to the Facebook shit list, Mrs. Minivan," he cackled like a lunatic. When he finally had room to straighten out and drive, he exhaled and accelerated. A blur from his right made him jam the brakes just in time to let two kids cross at a second unsanctioned area. As his gaze traced their slow-motion progress, a woman came racing toward him from behind, shaking her hand, screaming something.

"God, I'm moving. What else do you want? My first born? Today, I might give him to you."

He gave a sarcastic wave and smile and pulled clean away, determined to set his mind on the final step in purchasing his building. He'd even bought a celebratory overcoat for the occasion—something for good luck, for the big hurrah. He could finally afford to buy anything he wanted without a thought for whether it would impact the kids' college funds or upgrades and additions onto the Ebberts family home. That was an achievement that felt as good as he had imagined it would back when he'd had nothing.

He deserved to feel this success. He had worked hard. That's why he saw the new coat as a symbol of his achievements. He'd bought it in New York City while closing on a building on Park Avenue. After the deal was done, he'd sauntered down the street, so full of everything good. He'd never felt such incredible satisfaction. So high, he nearly floated past the men's boutique. But something made him look twice at the window and then stop cold.

The coat was being modeled on a live man. The unusualness of it, the obvious cashmere quality, the unique color-blocking, casual scarves sewn right into it, drew him into the store. It was nothing like the overcoats he owned, or like any overcoat he'd ever seen. And the man wearing it looked exactly like Elliot felt inside. Beautiful, kingly.

When the boutique owner slid the coat over Elliot's arms and adjusted it across his shoulders, Elliot felt a distinct shift inside. As high as he'd been when he walked in the door, his sense of pride ballooned even more now that he was wearing the garment.

"Ahh, yes. Perfect. This is a coat fit for a man of your substance and presence."

Elliot nodded. That was it. What had shifted was the full realization that he was no longer a poor, homeless boy wearing clothes people made fun of at a regular clip.

"You'll be surprised what a coat like this can do for a man. It speaks to your discerning taste that you came in to try it on."

"Yes." Elliot had felt its importance, its specialness in the same way he felt those things about himself. How far he'd come in life. The boutique owner was absolutely correct. It was as though the luxurious coat itself had compelled him to want it, to need it. And without a second of conflict, Elliot plunked down his Centurion card. Unfazed by the $4,879.00 price, he sauntered right out of the boutique elated.

Once home, he'd given it to Libby to wrap for him to open on Christmas morning. But then when she called to say she needed him to do drop-off, he felt a niggling, a prodding. Something inside told him he might need a shot of confidence that day. He couldn't imagine why that would be true, but he heeded the feeling. Although there was nothing concrete blocking the purchase of the building at that point, and it was a tiny acquisition compared to what he'd just bought in New York, a cranky cadre of do-gooders had expressed their dissatisfaction at his plans. And though they had no legal bearing to stop the sale, he wanted an extra layer of confidence while facing them one last time. He wanted that feeling he'd had in New York.

And so, that morning, Elliot had carefully unwrapped the coat in order to wear it to the meeting. He'd kept its details from Libby, knowing she thought anything bought outside of Target was ostentatious. Now that he was no longer in New York, no longer under the soft glow of the boutique lights and the owner's kind words, the price did make Elliot choke a little. A shot of nausea shook him—a remnant from childhood days when his father bought stale bread for suppers of cucumber butter sandwiches, when there was no money for the most basic expenses. Even the pants Elliot wore to high school graduation were given to him right off the backside of a man who saw future greatness in him and knew the importance of long pants on graduation day. Elliot had been so grateful that day. But now the thought of wearing Jimmy Bach's jeans under his graduation robe instead of chinos or dress pants purchased specifically for the occasion draped him in sadness. "Nothing extra, son. We can't manage it this week. We can't lose the car because you need fancy pants under your graduation robe. Those shorts'll do fine." His father had never understood the importance of dressing properly. And somehow the man found a way to pay his way into Pirates baseball games on a weekly basis—that, he had money for.

Elliot told himself to ignore his misgivings about the coat. He could afford to lose a whole car these days. He'd smoothed the front of the coat. Its fabric still held the scent of the boutique, the fresh whiff of accomplishment and wealth. And now he was part of that world, solidly somewhere he could ignore the voice that told him he shouldn't need the coat, that the promotion and bonus he'd just won were enough—the title, the extra money, the respect.

Once in Pittsburgh he waited to be waved into the parking lot a few blocks from Libby's old home. Many parts of East Liberty had recently been rejuvenated and were booming with new business. Others, like where Libby's home sat on Starflower Street, struggled.

He smiled at the thought of the reserved parking spot he'd been granted along with his promotion. In that garage, he'd be able to enter through a special door where there was never a line and certainly never a clutch of Facebook moms watching his every move, ready to report the latest parental carpool gaff. Silliness. He thanked God Libby's normal schedule allowed her to take care of the kids, that she didn't expect him to do it unless it was an emergency like this morning.

He pulled into an open parking spot and got out of the car. He stretched his neck side to side and opened the back door to grab his good luck coat.

Gone.

The cloudy morning darkened the car even with the interior light on, so he paused. Was he going crazy? The coat had been there. He had scolded Jeffery for leaning against it. One of the kids must have knocked it off. Stepped all over it? "Dammit."

He hopped into the car and swept his hands over the middle seat and the floor. His phone beeped, interrupting his search. Joseph Hampton. "Ready, bro? Where are you? You want to make your wife's Christmas dreams come true, right?"

Elliot's heart throbbed and his face flushed. *Had* he brought the coat? He must have left it at home. He shuffled toward the parking lot exit, replaying the morning. No. He remembered hanging it on the hook inside the car. Clem had mentioned it, that she had to step around it to get in. Jeffery. Elliot pushed his hand through his hair then ground his teeth. He shook his head. Another few messages from Joseph beeped through. God, couldn't anyone leave him alone?

He looked over his shoulder at the car. The coat had to be in it. He would check the third row when he was finished with the closing.

Someone slapped his back. Chuck McHenry. The president of the company. "I hear you're making your first real estate purchase as a gift. Shows you're in the big time. Enjoy it. We'll get this neighborhood cleaned up yet. One building at a time. I can imagine the look on your wife's face when you give her the paperwork."

Elliot smiled and nodded. That did lift his spirits. And he had more planned than just surprising her with a stack of documents.

"I know your final words before signing will assure the Neighbors for Responsible Revitalization that you have their best interests at heart. They'll sign. I know it. That's why I like you. You made the impossible, possible."

Elliot glanced back at the car one last time as though he would see some evidence of the coat through the dark tinted glass.

"Elliot?" McHenry said.

Silly. Elliot swallowed hard. He told himself not to see the missing coat as a bad omen, the way he used to see things when his only luck was bad luck. He had a fine, plaid sports coat on and he would have removed the overcoat when they went inside anyway. He reminded himself he'd risen to vice president with a just barely finished state college education, that his upbringing no longer defined him, that he was in charge of his destiny.

All of that was true. He'd outperformed every single limitation he'd been born with. And yet. The coat. He'd bought it before the apartment deal was final. He should have waited. And his stomach—the snarled twisting sensation confirmed that thought. He'd counted his chickens before they hatched and now it felt as though the eggs were all broken.

**

Elliot wouldn't recount the meeting; he wanted it out of his head. He'd closed the deal. But the tone of the transfer was unexpectedly hostile. He would've sworn on court Bibles that he'd ironed out any wrinkles in the plan ahead of time. But no. His luck had gone bad.

The coat. All it took was for him to misplace it. The lawyer who represents the Neighbors for Responsible Revitalization—the group selling the building—were mouthy and misinformed. The lawyer, Mrs. Berry, chased after him toward the parking lot, close on his heels like a bloodhound.

"Hey." She latched onto Elliot's arm before he could cross the boulevard. Wind and snow whipped, forcing the two of them to squint at each other. Gusts peeled her corkscrewed, red hair out of her hat and she fought to tuck the strands back up into the wool beanie. "I hope you're happy. A present for your wife? You just destroyed four families' lives to give one person some damn gift. A gift you're going to destroy? That apartment building is the only thing keeping…" Her words trailed off.

Elliot didn't owe this woman any more explanations. He'd made his case for how the neighborhood committee could use the money instead of trying to maintain a falling-down building where they received little rent, not nearly enough to keep up with the maintenance. The rest of her committee had been disgruntled, grumbling, not making eye contact, but in the end, they agreed to the deal.

Mrs. Berry's face bore all her tension, eyes bulging in her skull. "If you think for one second we give a damn that your wife grew up here, in the apartment on the top floor, and that her great-grandfather built it and… if you think that makes what you're doing all right, then—"

He waved her off and started walking again.

"I mean it. Her father would roll over in his cold grave if he knew you were doing this in her name. He was born in that house."

Elliot pulled back just before stepping off the curb and turned. "Mrs. Berry. Don't you dare pretend that this building, keeping it like it is, rotting and falling down, means anything to the neighborhood. Half the tenants are strung out and the other half are—"

She rushed him like a bull, pointing her mitten at him. Her dirty fingertips pushed through a hole in the seam and he wondered when was the last time she washed her hands. She pulled a long cardigan tighter around her midsection. She could not have looked less like a Harvard-educated lawyer than she did right then.

"You shut up." She bared her teeth. "You *shut up,* you pompous fool. You're like a giant baboon, trampling over ants, not even aware of what you're doing or who you're talking about. You…" Her eyes filled with tears. She looked away, struggling again with her hair that kept falling out of her worn hat, spiraling down her cheeks, then bouncing in front of her eyes.

He shook his head. What was he supposed to do? Maintain that building so people could live in it rent free, jobless, aimless? He simply didn't believe it helped anyone to live like that. He was doing them a favor by lighting a fire under them. Now they could reexamine their lives like he had when he realized he didn't want to mimic his father's life.

Mrs. Berry's intensity stunned him. She acted like she was one of the people living there. He despised her ruse, pretending she had more in common with the tenants than she did with him. Her threadbare clothing was part of her game—to look the part so none of the people she defended knew she was any better educated, paid, or situated than them. Her little act irritated him as much as the abject laziness of people who didn't bother to make their lives better.

He turned his back to Mrs. Berry.

"And two days before Christmas." She thumped his shoulder blade with her mittened fingers. "How dare you."

He shrugged and looked over his shoulder. Mrs. Berry's suddenly feeble, defeated, un-Harvard-like voice plucked at him. Maybe she did care about those people.

"I'm sorry." He adjusted his hat. Perhaps he owed her one more attempt at explaining he wasn't an ogre, that he had thought it through. "I don't think it makes a difference if it's today or the day after Christmas or New Years. Better for people to…"

She grabbed the collar of his sports coat. "Forty-five hundred dollars. You paid less than the cost of a car for a beautiful, old Victorian that houses several families in a neighborhood that just needs more time to thrive again. Just a little more time for the new energy of the business district to work its way over here."

He unlatched her hand from his coat, realizing he'd actually paid less for the property than he had for the coat—the one that was now missing. At least a building couldn't disappear when he wasn't looking.

"I have to—"

"No. You shut up. You go home to your wife and tell her what you just did. I'll bet she's not so proud of it. Unless she's like you now. Unless she's gone soulless since—"

Mrs. Berry's phone rang with the sound of a nuclear alarm. "I just wish you could understand." She lunged at Elliot and gripped his jacket so tight her hand shook as she pulled him close. "I wish—"

The phone sounded again, louder this time, and she released Elliot's coat, pulled out her phone and turned away from him.

He sighed and stepped into the street. See. She'd already moved on to her next project, finished thinking about him even when he was still standing right in front of her.

Now for that coat. He knew it was nuts, but he couldn't shake the feeling that because he had deemed it his lucky Christmas coat that misplacing it had turned everything darker.

**

Elliot phoned his secretary. She congratulated him, said there were no messages from anyone, that most people had left for the holidays and so he should definitely take the time to locate his lucky coat.

He got into his car and started the twenty-minute drive back to Oakmont to retrace his steps. Had he hallucinated Jeffery squashing the coat? Had he left it home after so carefully unwrapping it so he could put it back in the box when he returned from this meeting?

His phone rang and he answered.

"Elliot?"

"Lib, hey. Hi. Why aren't you sleeping? You've been up for twenty-four hours." The sound of her voice still warmed him after knowing her for twenty years. She was the one person he wanted to make proud.

"It's Christmas! You know I don't want to miss a second of it."

"Yeah, but…"

"You didn't take the bag of clothes to school with the kids."

He could hear the plastic rustling in the background.

"Oh, I…" He'd been so busy carefully unwrapping his coat that he'd forgotten, and apparently so had his kids.

"Hey, I need to be honest here. I took my coat out of the package because I wanted it for good luck for a deal today and…"

The background noise took on a tell-tale echo and he knew Libby had put him on speaker.

"Anyway, don't be mad. I'll wrap it back up. But… did I leave it at the house? Do you see it in the kitchen or something?"

He heard the slam of the clothes washer door and the twisting sound the dial made when turned to start.

"That overcoat you had me wrap?"

"Yeah, that one. I swear it was in the car and the drop-off circle was insane and…"

"Ohhhh," another voice came over the line.

"Who's that? Lib?"

"Cheryl, here, Elliot. I saw a coat in the circle."

"In the circle?" Elliot said.

"Yeah. Twelve cars ran it over and when I pulled up to it, I made Hannah take it into the office. We were second to last to drop off so I only had one car blowing the horn at me. I'm sure my mugshot and license plate number will be on Facebook by noon." She chuckled. "Anyway, I figured the coat was for the clothing drive since it was an adult size."

"Oh… No." Elliot ran his hand through his hair.

"But, it couldn't be yours, Elliot," Cheryl said. "The coat everyone was running over was a woman's coat. Beige and red and with fringy, scarffy things hanging off of it."

Silence swept over the connection.

Elliot's face reddened as though Cheryl was there with him to see that the coat was in fact his. And he hadn't thought it womanly at all, not in the least.

"I got that in a men's boutique."

"Boutique?" Cheryl and Libby said simultaneously.

"Yes, New York…" He sighed. "Never mind. I'm nearly back in Oakmont. I'll stop at the school."

**

Frigging Jeffery. He must have knocked it out when he exited the car with his giant backpack and garbage bag full of clothes for the drive. Elliot parked along the yellow-lined curb near the front door of the school. Every single spot was taken but he would just be a moment and couldn't afford to sit there waiting for someone to leave and open up a space. Enraged at the thought that his coat might be the casualty Cheryl described as being run over by a dozen cars, he wouldn't let himself imagine the slushy result. Besides, it couldn't be his coat because it was clearly cut for a man even if it deviated from the ordinary boring gray and black wool. My God, he was six foot four. What woman could possibly even fit into it?

He buzzed and buzzed the door, shifting his weight.

When he was finally granted access he entered the school office where secretaries and other support staff were smiling and munching on cookies. Holiday music played softly, obscuring the hallway noise as students changed classes, singing their own carols. The extreme jolliness only chafed Elliot's irritation more. How could these people be so grossly ecstatic?

He lifted his hand. "Um, hello. Hi."

They looked at him as though they'd never seen him before.

"Someone said a coat was turned in to the office. Cheryl Haden."

"Who are you?" asked a man holding plastic cups full of orange juice.

"Elliot Ebberts."

"Ohhh, Mr. Ebberts. It's been a while," the man with orange juice said. Elliot was too embarrassed to ask who he was. Elliot nodded. How long had it been since he'd been to the school?

"A coat," Elliot said. "Hannah Haden brought it into the office, I think."

"Oh, that ugly thing," the blonde secretary said. She said it with the calm analysis of a seasoned doctor sharing a diagnosis.

Elliot flinched, jaw clenched. "No. It's not..." He lifted his hands. "It's a man's overcoat. Cashmere."

The brunette secretary stepped to the front of the cluster. "Color-blocked thing? Felt like a million bucks. I was sort of surprised that it was intended for the clothing drive, despite it being..."

He exhaled. It was there. "Oh, thank God. Can I have it?"

The group passed glances and a third secretary still at her desk, paged through a book. "Stuff's already gone. Picked up two hours ago."

No. No. "Where?" He swallowed hard. The group studied him as though he'd asked for the location of a marijuana vending machine.

"Goodwill. East Liberty," the seated secretary said without looking up, sipping on a full cup of whip-creamed hot chocolate.

He held his breath. He'd just been there. The clothes probably passed him as he stood arguing with Mrs. Berry. Dammit.

Several students burst into the office holding presents over their heads. "For you, Mrs. Ritchie! And you…" They ticked off their list of people the gifts were for. Elliot knocked on the countertop that stood between him and school posse who now seemed to think he was nuts. "So Goodwill. On Centre?"

He barely got a yes from the crowd of people exchanging gifts. It was as though they didn't even care that his coat had gone missing.

CHAPTER 2

Mary Jane trudged home, despondent, not sure she could go through with it. Snow piled up, covering the woman's footsteps in front of her so quickly that she made fresh prints in their place. Perhaps the weather was reason enough for her to decline the invitation.

I wish I could face my daughter, my past, our past. No. I wish I could go back in time and change everything. Just do it all over.

She wasn't sure she could show up to the hospital even though she'd heard her daughter's voice on the message. This time it wasn't just her son-in-law calling, trying to bridge the gap between wife and mother-in-law. *She* asked Mary Jane to come. That petrified her and reassured her at the same time. So the latter was the feeling Mary Jane tried to convince herself to latch onto. She kept telling herself to put one foot in front of the other, show up and the rest would take care of itself. Sobriety had taught her that much.

At her apartment, she picked up the present she'd bought for her daughter's first child.

Mary Jane had wrapped it in newspaper but added the pink silk ribbon that came with a gift her sponsor had given her when she was three years sober. She'd saved it knowing the perfect chance to use it would arrive. She wouldn't have guessed a year back that this occasion would be doubly special—her first grandchild and her daughter inviting Mary Jane back into her life.

She ran a brush through her hair, then dug out lipstick so old that it crumbled when she drew it along her lips. She'd been diligent in changing her insides, confronting her alcoholic behaviors, and transforming how she responded to triggers, to life, to her very own breath some days. But she knew that part of showing her estranged daughter that she changed meant she needed to dress respectably. She paged through her closet. Everything was old. Not just unfashionable, but stained or torn or worn to translucence. Like she often felt when she woke, like her nerves and her soul were barely veiled, vulnerable to the world's abrasive elements.

She shook her head. No. This was not the time to feel sorry for herself, nervous as she was that her daughter would change her mind about letting her back in. What if she arrived at the hospital and then was turned away?

No. Don't do that to yourself. Mary Jane knew right then she had to buy something that would visually demonstrate she was sober, that she wasn't even a dry drunk. She was recovering and nearer to healthy than she'd ever been in her life. And she couldn't allow her daughter's first glimpse of her to be shrouded in clothes so awful they ought to be tossed away without a second thought.

**

Mary Jane entered Goodwill and stomped the snow from her boots. Christmas music played and a man sorting through plates and cups in the houseware section sang so loud she couldn't help but smile at his enthusiasm. He wasn't suffering any worries that day.

Mary Jane located the women's clothing section. She rifled through the racks, not having much time to get to the hospital for her designated timeslot to spend with her daughter, son-in-law, and their new baby. Every item seemed gaudy and bright, like things she might wear to a nightclub if she were looking to hook a man and take him home in a drunken haze… if she were twenty years younger. She sighed and turned slowly. Was she in the teen section?

A man dragging a rack of clothes went past her.

Coats. That's it. Her daughter had told her that she was welcome to spend half an hour at the hospital with them. That wasn't even enough time for anyone to expect her to remove her coat. That was it. She could cover up her clothes with something that would at least convey the distinctive sense of being sober, of being respectable. Perfect.

She ran after the man with the coats. "Can I look through those?"

"Haven't priced them yet."

"Please. I just need something to wear over my sweater and jeans and…" She was already paging through the rack. All the coats were cut slim and none squeezed over her rugged sweater or covered the jeans.

The man eyed her up and down. "Go there. The men's section."

She narrowed her eyes on him.

"Trust me. I just priced and hung a bunch of coats. One…" He took her by the arm, leading her. "One of them… well, I can't believe I'm telling you this, but one of them had the tag in the pocket. Said the thing cost four thousand some dollars."

She flinched. "Seriously?"

He scrolled through the hangers. "But it's so flashy. I considered selling it on eBay, except that's against our rules and well… here."

He pulled the coat from the rack. "Feel this. Cashmere. It's more suited for a woman, and if you want that bulky sweater underneath… I know it's long and it was dirty, but I cleaned it off and…"

She eyed it. The loud color blocks would draw attention. She was more accustomed to… more *comfortable* with disappearing into her surroundings. "No."

"Just try it."

She took the coat from him and slipped it over her shoulders. It was roomy for sure, but the casual, low slung shoulder seams effortlessly covered her rugged, old clothing. Basically, somehow, it fit. It nearly dusted the tops of her shoes, but that was perfect. She belted it and he took her to the mirror. She was slim, but tall enough that it almost looked purposeful, the crazy color blocking, the fringy scarves that hung off it. "This is a man's coat?"

The clerk grabbed her shoulders. "A forty-eight-hundred-dollar men's coat."

She shook her head. "Well… no. I'm sure I can't afford it."

"It's thirty-five bucks. No way was I going to sell it for more. Our clientele..." He shut his mouth.

She patted the young man's hand and nodded. "It's okay. I'm your clientele and I know it."

"Well. Wherever it is that you're going in that coat, you'll kill it." He snapped his fingers in front of his face.

She looked at her appearance in the mirror, ran her fingers through her hair, saw that the old lipstick had given her just enough color to not appear corpse-like. She sighed. The man was right. It would do perfectly. And so she took thirty-five of her last hundred dollars, paid, and headed for the hospital.

**

Mary Jane entered the elevator to the maternity ward and gasped. Catching her reflection in the mirror, she thought she was looking at an image of her from a decade back. How long had it been since her appearance, her look, caused her to feel proud? She pulled the belt tighter to settle the quivering belly nerves that were telling her she had no right to feel such confidence.

When she entered her daughter's room, the look on Caroline's face said everything Mary Jane had been afraid it wouldn't. Her daughter's expression was soft and loving, pink like the little bundle in her arms.

Still standing near the doorway, Mary Jane smoothed the coat and then balled the ends of the belt in her hand. The cashmere, like a baby's blanket, calmed her like a child.

"Come close, Momma."

Caroline's words, the tenderness in them, caused Mary Jane's eyes to well then practically spurt.

"Oh, my. I'm sorry." She wiped her cheeks with the back of one hand. "I didn't..."

Caroline shifted in the bed and gestured. "Come see her."

And so Mary Jane swallowed her tears of relief and appreciation and awe at the idea that her daughter was granting her a thirty-third chance at being a mother, a first chance at being a grandmother.

"Well, hello there, stranger," Henry, Caroline's husband, said as he slipped into the room.

Mary Jane nodded her greeting, studying his face, basking in his kindness. She handed him the present which he set on the counter.

He slipped his arm around her and tried to move toward Caroline. When Mary Jane didn't budge, still stunned that she was there with her family, that there was still such a thing she could consider to be that, Henry patted her on the back. "What? You don't want to hold sweet Mary?"

Her knees weakened and Henry caught her as she quaked. She had to force herself to meet Caroline's gaze. "Mary?" she said through a whisper.

Caroline nodded. "Yes. Mary. After you."

**

Mary Jane visited with her family for nearly an hour and then as Caroline and the baby fell into peaceful sleep and Henry took a work call, she slipped out, not wanting to disturb the perfection of her reentry into her daughter's life. She knew it would take a lot more to really prove that she was no longer swinging between a raging, angry drunk and a sniveling, helpless, curled-in-a-ball weakling. But she was grateful that Henry had kept an eye on her progress, that he helped smooth the path of mother back to daughter.

She headed home to her apartment and felt a stab of disappointment. Alone again. Togetherness had been fleeting. To deal with that, the thought that she ought to stop in Murphy's Pub for a beer and sandwich to celebrate came to mind and made her stop dead. She twisted her hair into a knot at the nape of her neck, shocked at the ease with which the idea of beer just tumbled back into her head. She pressed her belly with both hands, assessing the lure of drinking at that moment. That's where the desire always started for her, in her stomach—the demand to be warmed and filled with liquid happiness.

She stood there in the wind, stunned for a second time. She played the movie forward, how the pleasant first alcohol-infused moments would be precious and then as ugly and dark as she could imagine. And with that, the temptation dissolved as fast as it had arrived. She marveled that she at last could have the thought to honor progress with a drink, but not have to follow it to a bar and drink herself half-dead.

The odd weight of believing that she had truly changed, feeling it, turned her woozy, made her sit on the bench at the bus stop near her apartment. Her breath returned with a smile. She was truly changing. She smoothed the coat, thinking that she ought to list it on eBay and sell it. Forty-eight hundred dollars? Who on earth would spend that on a coat? An ugly one at that. But... she ran her hands down the front of it again. It had lent her the air of "okayness" that she had needed to actually show up at the hospital. Like magic. It happened. Real as anything. That, she couldn't deny.

She eyed the man beside her. He closed a briefcase and sighed, his leg bouncing, clearly nervous.

"You all right?" she asked.

He nodded, looking at her, then away.

"Good, good," she said.

The man shifted, looking right at Mary Jane. "Interview. Riverhouse Digital. First one in a long time. Long time."

Snow began to fall again, catching on his eyelashes. He wore a kind expression and when he explained his doubts about getting the job, and how badly he needed it, Mary Jane nodded along. "I know exactly how you feel."

"I just wish I could get this one and keep it. That's the trick, you know." He wiggled his eyebrows at her. "Keeping the job's the hard part."

Mary Jane nodded and chuckled. "Yeah, that damn having to follow through thing always is."

A bus stopped three lights away and he stood.

His shoulders slumped and the khaki pants drooped at his bottom. "I don't know why I told you all that. I usually go four days without a word to anyone including the cashier at Giant Eagle. But thanks. For the talk."

She stood and untied the coat. "Here. Take this."

He flinched. "What?"

She took the belt off the coat and put it into the pocket. "It's a man's coat. I just bought it for a song two hours ago."

He stared at her and then the coat. "No way. That's…"

"Ugly as the devil, I know. But it's worth… well, that doesn't matter, but I'm telling you. It's cashmere and I swear it's a man's coat. Just let it hang casually and…"

She held it open.

He cocked his head.

"I mean it. Just wear it and you'll see. It does something… I don't know. Just try it."

"Like magic tricks?"

She chuckled. It felt that way to her. "Sort of. A Christmas coat. Magic. Yes. But no. Of course that's silly."

He set his briefcase down. "Of course." He narrowed his gaze on her then looked over his shoulder at the approaching bus. "All right. What do I have to lose by wearing a womanly man's coat… except any sense of manhood I might possess after a year of abject depression and unemployment?"

"Well, if the men at Riverhouse Digital are as savvy as I hear, they'll note the quality cashmere and forgive you the fringy scarf things."

He squinted at her again.

"Well, here. Let's do this. Hold it for me."

She dug into her giant satchel and pulled out shears. "Never know when I'll need these." Her tongue protruded at the corner of her mouth as she concentrated and cut along bottom of the dangling scarves, removing the fringy ends and tucking them into her purse as the bus pulled up. Mary Jane helped him into the coat and brushed lint from the shoulders. The two of them grinned at each other and Mary Jane felt as though she'd known him forever. She felt strange that she wouldn't be seeing him later, that she'd never know how his interview went.

He climbed onto the bus and turned before the doors shut, arms spread, face bright. "You're right. I feel like a million bucks."

She nodded. "Well, four thousand, eight hundred anyway."

He grabbed the railings and leaned forward, laughing as the door shut. "No way. Really?"

She lifted her hand to him, laughing. "Yes, way."

When the bus was gone she looked down. Her ten-year-old jeans and sweater made her feel like Cinderella after midnight. Gone was the confidence, the calm, the comfort of the stunning, yet ugly, Christmas coat.

She started back toward her apartment at a slow trudge. But then she stopped. She stared into the sky, the pewter heavens dropping sparkling snowflakes like rain. The sun, obscured, still shone, still strong enough to make her shade her eyes with her hand. The beauty of the scene, the scent of Christmas pine being sold on the corner and the snow, its blanketing effect, hushing the city noise reestablished the contentment the coat had offered.

She ran her fingers over the expensive cashmere fringe in her purse then slung the strap over her shoulder. None of what she'd felt with the coat was gone after all. Mary. *Her granddaughter bore her name.* And that was all she needed to keep her warm, to spark joy, to remind her that she had really changed her life.

CHAPTER 3

Elliot rushed into the Goodwill, slipping as he turned the corner to approach the cashier at the register. Anger. He chewed on bitterness that instead of celebrating the purchase of the apartment building for Libby, he was laser focused on the coat. Other than it being his hard-earned coat, he was determined to get it back just to prove to himself that it wasn't ugly and it certainly wasn't a woman's coat.

"'Scuse me."

The cashier held up one finger and finished counting cash and recording something in a book. Finally she turned her attention to Elliot.

"Please. There was a delivery of clothing from a school. Just a couple of hours back." He put his thumb over his shoulder. A coat got mixed up in the bunch and it wasn't supposed to end up here. It's not supposed to be here. It's very important. It's…"

The cashier sighed with her whole body. "Third one today." She jerked her head toward the front corner of the store and snapped her chewing gum. A woman sat in a chair near an office door, head bowed in her hands, obviously crying.

"What? Third one, what?" Elliot wasn't sure what the cashier was getting at.

She leaned forward putting one hand to her mouth to signify a secret. "Husband brought in a vase. Ming Dynasty. Her father brought it back from some… I don't know. But you get the point. Happens every day. Stuff shows up here by accident."

"Mine's a coat. Please. I'll go through the bags if you want. Just please…"

She waved her hand at him. "A coat. Oh, that's good. At least you won't be crying in the corner over a coat." She flashed a smile, her green gum pushing through two teeth.

"Not if I get it back."

"Cute." She wiggled her eyebrows.

"Please. I won't put you out. I'll go through the bags. It's a coat, red and beige sections of color and…"

"The forty-eight-hundred seventy-nine-dollar coat?" A twenty-something man slunk toward Elliot and the cashier. He was wearing a Goodwill smock.

Elliot moved toward him. "You know it? Yes. Please. That one."

The man in the smock glanced at the cashier and Elliot caught their awkward smiles.

"What?" Elliot said.

"Gone." The man lifted his hands.

Elliot's belly clenched. Impossible. "But it just got here. Right? You sure that's the… From Riverview High School—the clothing drive. The stuff can't even be unpacked let alone anything sold."

The man pursed his lips. "We work fast, hard, efficiently here, sir."

"But *sold?* Can I look? You can't be right." What a disaster of a day. Was this really happening to him?

The man brushed his mustache with his finger and thumb. "Gonzo."

Elliot brushed the sweat that burst from his hairline. His stomach churned with panic. He shook his head. No. It was too crazy to be true. "You're sure we're talking about the same coat?" He started pounding on his phone, calling up the boutique website and a photo of the coat. He turned the screen to the man and the cashier. "This?"

The two employees nodded. "Yeppers," the cashier said.

Elliot's vision blurred. "Oh, my God."

"You really paid forty-eight hundred bucks for that?"

He nodded, his breath thinning in his chest. This coat was everything to him. The quality, the fact that it was expensively casual and signified that he could buy something, something decadent and unneeded, without a thought after the way he'd been raised, was everything. And the reassurance of his success that he'd felt in the store when he put it on, when the owner of the boutique exclaimed at his handsomeness when wearing it. It all had combined to make the purchase more than just something expensive.

"I thought it was a mistake, like a different tag got into the pocket," the mustached clerk said.

Elliot put his hand to his chest. "Who bought it? Wasn't it dirty? Apparently it had been run over in the street like roadkill or…"

"Cleaned up beautifully." The clerk leaned against the counter and the cashier nodded in agreement. "I wiped it down and brushed it and… weird how easily it shaped up, now that I think about it. Almost like…" He shrugged. "Yeah. Good as new."

"Who bought it? Surely the guy can't just keep it if it was sold by accident."

"Oh yes, he can," the cashier said.

The clerk nodded sympathetically. "There are no accidents at the Goodwill. Destiny, my man."

"But, he'll sell it back to me surely. Once he hears that I didn't mean—"

The cashier swiped her hand through the air with a snap. "It was a chick."

"It was a chick, what? What does that mean?"

"A lady, really. Not a chick as in young," the clerk said. "She needed a coat for something…" He shook his finger then tapped it against his lips while he thought. "Her daughter. That's it. Had to see her and the new grandbaby at the hospital and… she seemed sad. Like… well, all teary-eyed and…" He mimed her putting on the coat. "She slipped that coat on and her whole posture changed. I felt like a fairy godmother or something. It was perfect. On it went and suddenly she glowed. Confidence. Magic."

"Oh, really." Elliot's tone was sarcastic.

"And all for thirty-five dollars." The cashier nodded.

Elliot gripped the cashier's counter. "Oh, dear God. You sold it for… Well then, please, give me her name, her address. I'll pay double to get it back."

The two employees passed another uncomfortable glance between them. "We can't just give you her private information."

Elliot scanned the counter, eyeing the open book where the cashier had been writing. It was a list of names and addresses.

The cashier tried to grab it. "That's our mailing list for when things come in that we know customers might like based on their purchasing habits."

Elliot stepped away from the counter, reading aloud. "Ugly color-block coat. MJ Berry."

He stared at the name. Berry. Mrs. Berry. What was that lawyer's first name? He couldn't remember. Odd. Then he noticed the address. It was the apartment building he'd just bought. He scratched his cheek. What was going on? It couldn't be her. Had she known the coat was his? Had he mentioned that it was missing at the meeting? Was she stalking him? Using the building he bought as a drop-off for... what? Now he was irate. That woman not only treated him unfairly, but was stalking him. He would put an end to that.

"You said she went to see her new grandbaby?"

"Yep. West Penn Hospital," the clerk said.

And Elliot took off for there.

CHAPTER 4

Jonathan Gray exited Riverhouse Digital in a daze. He pulled his sunglasses out of his briefcase. Head thrown back, he watched silver dollar snowflakes dump from a silver sky, brightening, glistening as silver sunrays hit them. He didn't know what to make of it. The numbing, black depression that had embedded itself in his bones three years before was still there. He would have been out of touch with reality to believe the coat was anything more than an oddly crafted garment, overly expensive, castoff by some lady he met at the bus stop who thought it gave her confidence to face her past... confidence she hadn't had until she'd put it on. He may have been emotionally struggling and depressed, but he was not delusional.

And yet.

His eyes burned at the corners. A crack in the sludge that had kept him from feeling anything for so many years opened up, letting it all in or out or... he couldn't say, but for the first time in so long he was feeling *something*. Confusion choked him.

No. He would not let this sensation, the ability to actually feel discomfort, dissuade him from his path.

His mind flew to his parents back in Fresno. They'd kept his bank account stocked, but the money that flowed from them to him never did a thing to lift him out of the depression that kept him from holding a job. He didn't need money. He needed purpose. And apparently a freakishly weird coat.

He'd been given the job. And inside him, somewhere at the center of the darkness was a seed of... something... he couldn't define it or label it but it was there. For the first time he thought somehow he might keep this job. He wasn't going to screw it up.

He looked down the road to the left. The red brick building was so familiar. Her office. His therapist, the one he'd been avoiding for six months, had said he could buzz in and wait for an appointment any time.

A tear pushed over the lid of one eye and trailed down his wind-stung cheek. What was happening? He brushed one hand over the front of the soft coat.

A nice woman at just the right time. A magic Christmas coat. Preposterous.

He eyed the brick building again. He went down the stairs to the sidewalk and took one step in that direction and then another. No coat would keep him from losing another job. Only he could do that. And so he headed for the building, hoping his therapist would be there.

CHAPTER 5

Elliot lucked out getting a parking spot on Friendship Avenue right outside the hospital entrance. He'd picked Libby up from work enough times back when they were newly married that the labyrinth of hallways and elevators to Labor and Delivery didn't daunt him at all.

When he approached the desk on the fifth floor he knew he'd be stopped since he was not there to actually visit a patient. He ran a hand through his hair, trying to slow his breathing and convey a sense of normalcy, but a glance in the elevator mirror showed a wild-eyed man who should be steered away from the delicate happenings of maternity.

He almost stayed on the elevator when it stopped on floor five. What was he doing? He could track Mrs. Berry back to the apartment building. Apparently she was using it as her address for the store's list. What if this MJ wasn't the Harvard-educated extraordinaire who'd been harassing him for months?

"Elliot?"

He snapped his attention to the woman at the desk in front of the elevator.

"You're here. I didn't realize Libby sent you to pick this up." She held a large envelope and shook it at him.

"What?" He stepped into the hall and approached Sandra Lewis.

"She forgot this paperwork when she left and said to just hold it until her next shift… but here you are, you nice husband, you."

He tried to cover up his confusion. "Okay. Yes. Thank you."

He took the envelope and looked at it. The return address was from the imaging department. Libby had mentioned she was interested in applying for other jobs in the hospital, maybe getting onto a nine-to-five schedule… this must have something to do with that. His first thought was a new schedule might mean he'd be delegated to drop-off more often. *No. Please no.* He should just leave, but when he thought of the coat, its price, what it meant to him… he couldn't stop himself.

"Sandra. There's a Mrs. Berry. A woman I know is here… or was here or…"

She narrowed her eyes on him. He knew she couldn't tell him anything about patients.

"No. She's not a patient. Her daughter's here. We work together on a project…" He thought of how Mrs. Berry spit her words at him that morning, accusing him of throwing people out into the street. "Anyway, she borrowed a coat… it had big blocks of color… Cashmere…"

A slow smile slid across Sandra's face and she leaned forward on her forearms. "Oh, yes. Lovely woman. It's a miracle really."

"What's a miracle?"

Sandra cocked her head quizzically.

"Oh, birth. Her granddaughter. Yes, always a miracle."

"No. I mean the whole thing with her daughter and the grandbaby and Mrs. Berry's recovery and… the story was really incredible. Spoke to her on her way out after she visited. Full of tears and joy and… well it *is* Christmas. The official time for miracles."

This couldn't be the same Mrs. Berry he knew. A miracle? She was a menace.

"She almost didn't come to see her daughter. Been years since they spoke more than a few sentences here or there and then… she just kept staring at herself in the elevator doors and she turned and waltzed like the queen of England down the hall."

He bit the inside of his cheek, thoroughly confused.

Sandra leaned forward, lowering her voice to a whisper. "When she got into the room they told her they named the baby after her." Sandra's eyes were filling.

Elliot drew back. He wanted to tell Sandra he had no idea what she was talking about, that the Mrs. Berry he knew was a bull. She'd practically horned him in the chest at the closing just a few hours before.

"But the coat? Was this woman wearing the… here… let me show you." He plugged in the website and showed her the boutique's photo.

"That's it. Can't really unsee that." Her tone was mocking.

Elliot bit off the irritation that threatened to be expressed. How was it all these people saw the coat as something unattractive?

"Isn't it amazing how a person can turn her life around and how people can be forgiving and…"

He nodded, pretending he understood what this meant relative to this MJ Berry. He certainly understood what it meant in relation to his own father. Words like "recovery" took Elliot back in time to places he didn't want to go with people he didn't want to think about.

She waved him off. "Well, I don't have to tell you. I'm sure you know the whole story."

He nodded and looked at the envelope in his hand.

The phone rang and Sandra picked it up.

"I better get going." Elliot slipped away and pounded on the elevator call button.

**

In his car, he set the envelope on the passenger seat. He started to drive away but the phone rang.

"Libby, honey. Hey, I just—"

"What the freaking hell, Elliot? Tell me this isn't true."

Could Sandra have alerted Libby to him showing up at the hospital already? "Oh I know, I just—"

"You just what? Decided we have a spare four thousand eight hundred seventy-nine bucks to spend on a *coat?*"

The light turned green and he accelerated. "Wait… How did you…"

"Oh, don't worry. I didn't snoop into your little receipt book, if that's what you're thinking. Cheryl and I googled the damn coat after we got off the phone with you and… How *could* you?"

"Wait. Wait—"

"And now the freaking thing is *LOST*? Are you kidding me?"

"I'm going to find it. I know where it is. I just…"

"That's not the point. It's that you would spend so much money when we need it."

"We don't need it. I know it's extravagant. But I've told you before about…"

"Yes. You explained why you buy thousand-dollar suits because you have low self-esteem and how the girls at school used to mock your clothes and you wore sweatpants to your interview for college and somehow they miraculously let you in despite that, and how bad it…"

She stopped ranting, stopped short of reminding him that he'd even lived in his car at one point. He thought he heard a catch in her breath like it sounds when someone is holding back a sob.

"Libby. Please. Why are you this angry about…"

"You didn't even take the clothes to the clothing drive. And I heard about you shooting the finger to the whole drop-off line, swearing at people like a lunatic."

"I didn't swear, I swear I didn't."

She sighed.

"The finger? Yes. Guilty, but you should have seen it. These people were gnashing their teeth at me and glaring and laying on the horn, gesturing, and—"

"Elliot." She cut him off. "There are people who need things that we can just easily give away—the clothes in the bag. But you were too busy sneaking that coat out of the Christmas packaging for what? Just to lose the stupid thing?"

"For my meeting. I needed it for good luck."

"What? What the hell does that mean?"

"It's…" He wanted to tell her about the present he bought her for Christmas—the apartment building, her old home, that he'd been brutally savaged by the Residents for Responsible Restoration and their ringleader, Mrs. Berry. Unfairly so. But anger replaced his defensiveness. "Just stop. I made a ton of money on this last deal in New York. I wouldn't have bought that coat or the…"

"The what?"

The line beeped. "It's the hospital," Libby said, and Elliot thought he could hear a sniffle in her voice. Was she *crying*?

"So selfish of you and…"

"Wait—"

The line clicked dead.

His heart pounded, making him short of breath. Damn coat. When he'd slipped it on in that boutique he could never have imagined it would cause so much trouble. What an awful thing it was turning out to be. "I'll return the coat if it means that much to you," he said to no one.

He pulled the car over and laid his head against the wheel. What was he doing? Was its purchase really that unreasonable? He told her he'd made a lot of money that month. She was excited for him, but not impressed. Maybe he didn't tell her how much money? Her words stung. Noting his self-consciousness. They'd talked about it many times over the years. But he was long over that, wasn't he? Did Libby still see him as an insecure man trying to make his way in the world? The man with the shy, drunk, ineffective father who crumbled when his mother left them, leaving Elliot to fend for himself most of the time, to depend on sporadic gifts from adults who happened into his life from time to time.

Libby's anger cut through him. Was she leaving him? The thought was in his head unbidden and his body reacted by bursting into sweat. His stomach tightened and he felt acid release, his marker for true stress. He'd worked so hard at crafting his life to never feel that slow burning that fed his panic and obsession. He hadn't thought of his mother in ages. But the sense of abandonment appeared inside him, out of nowhere, just like the coat.

He gripped the steering wheel. No. Libby was nothing like Elliot's mother. But she had left him and his father out of sheer boredom. If someone could leave her son and husband for that pitiful reason, surely… no. That was insane. Just because Libby sounded irate when she had no reason did not mean his world was shattering. He was not his father. Libby was not his mother.

He reminded himself of the apartment building. He'd arranged to have his secretary and a handyman string the place with lights, add potted pines and wreaths so when he took Libby and the kids to see it, the vision would be a life-size embodiment of a true gift, a symbol of their family success. Mostly, it signified security. If they owned things, that meant they were layers and layers away from living in their car. His plan to tear the place down and rebuild a sleek, accessible-to-young-professionals, apartment building was a good thing, a contribution to society. And Libby would be proud of her old neighborhood again. And she would be proud of Elliot.

**

He felt shame about the coat, now. Somehow the luxurious garment was making him feel as bad as when his clothing was threadbare, too short and too tight, when he and his father had been homeless. How was that even possible?

Elliot turned his thoughts back to the coat and Mrs. Berry. He pulled up in front of Libby's old home and hopped out of the car. He looked at the peeling paint, the once striking colors, pinks and blues now faded and curling away from the wood. He envisioned it as it had been when cared for properly, when Libby lived there, happy and content. It wasn't as though her family had been wealthy. Difference was, she had an intact family who loved her, who put each other first. She never felt abandonment or hunger even if they had struggled at times.

He pounded on the ugly security door that had been added at some point, keeping people who didn't live there, out. But he owned the thing, dammit . He dug through his pockets for the keys he'd been given at the closing. He looked at them in the palm of his hand. He was not supposed to enter yet. Part of the deal he signed was to allow the tenants to stay in their apartments until the first of the year. So, instead of entering, he pounded on the door and rang each and every button.

"Broken. Get lost. New owner'll fix it."

The voice came from above, but the porch roof blocked Elliot's view of the person yelling out the window. He backed away from the building and shaded his eyes.

"You," the voice came again, but the face was blotted out by the sun. He knew the spitting, spiteful voice.

"*You*," he said. "What're you doing in my building?"

"Living. You've heard of it, right?"

He paused. "You never said you were a tenant."

The window slammed shut and the sound of feet pounding down stairs filled Elliot's ears. He held his breath half expecting her to come at him with a steak knife.

She burst out of the building. "New Year's Day isn't awful enough to kick us all out? You're here to push us out now?"

Elliot's mind filled with all the stuff Sandra had told him at the hospital. He eyed Mrs. Berry's clothing, the same tattered things she'd been wearing that morning at the closing. He'd silently accused her of dressing down in order to appear poor and defeated. Was it possible she actually was all that? *Recovery.* Hadn't seen her daughter in years. His heart stuttered. Was it possible she actually lived in his building like a pauper?

"No. It's not that. I..." It was none of his business and frankly he didn't want to know her troubles. He didn't need to pull them up under his chin along with his own issues and worries. Heck, until that day he'd managed to submerge all things negative in his memory, in his life, into the muck under his feet. Until now. Now it was rising into his pantlegs like quicksand, like he hadn't realized he'd stored his ugly past right inside his shoes. Though the sun shone gold and bright, it was still snowing. Tiny, pinprick flakes fell fast and thick.

"I need the coat," he said.

She crossed her arms. Her red hair whipped in the wind and she tucked a piece behind her ear. There it was, her indignance. The story Sandra told him didn't make sense at all. Were they talking about two different people? "Coat?" She tapped her foot, pursed her lips.

"Yeah. Goodwill, the cashmere coat that they shouldn't have sold but did."

"What makes you think I'd shop at Goodwill?"

He let out a puff of air. "I saw your name in the book they keep for their mailing list. They just let it sit there, open to the public, you know."

She slumped. "Damn, Goodwill and their archaic record keeping. I knew I shouldn't have put my name down."

Her defeat gave him a surge of good feelings. He reached into his sports coat pocket, pulled out a hundred-dollar bill, and held it out to her.

She scoffed.

The wind flapped one end of the bill. She snatched it and stuffed it into her jeans pocket.

"So, the coat."

"Gone."

"I'll wait." He opened his arms. "Go up and get it."

She shook her head.

"What the hell does that mean?"

"I gave the coat to someone who needed it more than me."

He choked. "You what?"

"Someone needed a little lift. A little confidence."

"And you used my coat to deliver a little bit of confidence? Just," he shrugged, "gave it away like it was nothing?" His anger swelled.

She studied him for a moment and he waited for her to blast him with witty barbs. She sighed. "I know, I know. Generosity's foreign to you." She looked down on him like he was a poorly behaved child.

"That's…" His voice cracked. He cleared his throat and wiped his brow with his forearm, heat filling him. "That's absolutely false."

She leaned on one hip. "You paid three hundred more dollars for that ugly, albeit, magical coat than you did for my home—this building." She swung her arm toward the old Victorian like she was hosting *The Price is Right*. "And then you're going to just tear it down without a thought." She caught a snowflake on her palm. "Oh, look at that," she said.

They both leaned in to see better. For a few moments every slope and angle of the stunning little flake held true to itself. But then her warm skin melted it, collapsing it into a humble waterdrop.

She looked at him, standing so close he could see that her brown eyes held greens and even blues when the sun shone.

She held her hand up to him. "Like that snowflake, Elliot. That magnificent snowflake is gone like it was never here. The building is the same. Gone in an instant." She frowned.

He studied her eyes some more, one having red veining and the other bright white. Her coldness forced a chill up his spine and he backed away. "You say that like an accusation."

"Think about it."

Oh, he'd thought about it. He knew what she meant. But he didn't accept that somehow his plans were a selfish act of greed, that building something new meant that the older building had never been there. "Don't act like I'm some snob and you're some guttersnipe. You went to Harvard and if you're living this way it's your doing, not mine. This hovel—"

"This hovel's my home and home to several families. Don't you dare condescend. You've no idea what I've been through, and yes, my Harvard education is the only thing… the *only* thread that ties me to my former life of success and ease and… Well, until today, that is… and if not for that education, I'd be…" She swallowed hard, her neck tensing. "Don't assume you know anything important about me or the people who live here. Don't pretend that you understand what it's like to have nothing."

"I just—"

She covered his mouth with her hand. "All you need to know is that you're taking the last sliver of stability that a particular set of people have and yanking it right out from under them. That's all you need to know. You are ruining people's lives."

"I need to know—"

She dropped her hand. "The fella I gave the coat to had an interview at Riverhouse Digital. I'm sure someone there has his address."

And with that she turned to the door and put the key into the lock.

"Hey. Give me my hundy back," Elliot said.

She looked over her shoulder, fiddling with the lock. "No way."

"It's mine."

"Consider it an asshole tax."

He grimaced. How was it every stinking person with no money just decided everyone with money was automatically an asshole?

"I'm not!" he said as she disappeared into the apartment building, his building. "I'm not an asshole."

But he was in pain. Oh, he knew what it was like to have nothing. He simply had put that part of his life behind him. He'd made good decisions and the result was no one was selling his home out from under him. Yet. The pinch that came with feeling like he had nothing, returned after a decade of abundance. The pinch deepened and widened, spreading through him, like February maple syrup pushing out of the tree bark. The pulsing brought back fear. He gripped his chest. The pain had been long missing but wasn't alien. The sensation of loss and hopelessness hit him like the bricks of this building would hit the ground when it was razed. And he couldn't breathe. He fought to get breath back into his lungs. Panic. It was coursing through him, taking him back in time to when his father would be gone for days and the store of canned goods in the glovebox had dwindled to nothing.

A window flew open above and Mary Jane stuck her head out, holding a steaming mug of something. Was she going to dump it on him? He started to back away, grabbing the banister as he nearly stumbled down the stairs.

"Wait," she said.

He stopped.

"I shouldn't have said you're an asshole. But you aren't even trying to understand or hear other people's limitations when it comes to 'just finding another place to live'." She made air quotes with her free hand. "You even act like you didn't know I lived here. Like you hadn't even been there for when we…"

He flinched. He hadn't known where she lived until that day. Certainly it had become clear to him that she must have mentioned at some point at one of the meetings that she was not only the lawyer for the community group trying to keep the building as a low-income rental, but that she too lived there. But he honestly hadn't heard that part. Had he been typing away on his computer when it was mentioned? He did tend to tune out when that shrill group listed their grievances. The list was long and deep. How many times did he have to hear that things were rough for the tenants and that they might have trouble finding new housing? He remembered explaining that when life was hard that reevaluating one's path usually helped. He recoiled at the thought. Had he said that? The words felt familiar, but right then in that context they felt so very wrong.

"Want some coffee?" She lifted the mug.

The question stung him. No, he didn't want coffee. Least of all coffee with her. "I have to… I've gotta go find that coat."

She nodded. "Well, I'm here if you want coffee later. You look like you need a friend. Or something."

He growled at her and waved his hand through the air. "Friend? I don't need anything except—"

And she disappeared, slamming the window shut.

Why in the hell would he want anything from her… ever? Friend? Was she certifiable? He would never consider being friends with her, someone like her. Especially not with the rude way she'd treated him every single time they met up. Friends. Ridiculous.

CHAPTER 6

Elliot trudged back to his car thinking about Mary Jane. He choked on her accusation. Had she revealed in one of their meetings that she lived in the building? He thought back to what she'd said right after the closing when she chased him down, ranting about Libby, how her father would roll over in his grave… did Mary Jane know Libby?

What difference did it make? The woman, though obviously downtrodden at the moment, was choosing to live a minimalist lifestyle and for that she only had herself to blame. God, he choked on his anger at how his day had gone. He looked in the rearview mirror and noticed his eyes were bloodshot like Mrs. Berry's had been. He looked disheveled. He felt disheveled, as though he'd been under someone's boot all day long. He reminded himself of his successful closing. That was what he should focus on. He would get the coat back and do just that.

He closed his eyes and took a few deep cleansing breaths the way everyone was always yakking about as an antidote to stress. In and out. *Okay, okay.* That's better. In and out. Better yet. In and out. Great. He was calm.

He punched "Riverhouse Digital" into his GPS. *I'll get my coat back and everything will fall back into place.* One thing at a time. That was the only way to proceed. The search pulled up the address, but he noticed a little red sentence indicating the business was only going to be open for another twenty minutes. Panic returned, yet as he screeched away, he saw his secretary and the workmen arriving, a truck full to bursting with Christmas decorations for the building. Oh, good. Decorations. At least that part was in hand and underway.

He couldn't wait to show Libby. That would change everything about this awful day. She would understand he only had good motives when it came to their family. All this stress over nothing would melt from his life like the little snowflake in Mary Jane Berry's palm.

Libby. Thinking of impressing her reminded him that she was angry. Unfairly so. He knew she didn't like his expensive wardrobe, but there was something more behind today's explosion. For now, all he wanted was to get the coat back and return it to the store. At least then Libby might speak to him. She had hung up on him. When was the last time she'd done that? When they were twenty years old? Yes. Officially giving her the building later that night after dinner would set everything wrong, right again.

Stuck at a long light, Elliot looked around for traffic and cops. He dug his fingers into his hair. *Please turn green. Just turn.* When it didn't, he checked in every direction again. Seeing no traffic or police, he tore through the red light. He had to get to the business. Tomorrow was Christmas Eve and their office would probably be closed. He needed his coat back right away.

He took the stairs to the lobby of Riverhouse Digital two at a time and burst inside. Three men were walking toward the exit, smiling, arms laden with ribboned boxes. When they waltzed right past Elliot, he sprinted to get back in front of them.

He held his hands up, breathing heavy. "Wait, wait, wait. You guys look official. Was there a man here for an interview? Wearing a really, really nice coat? Expensive coat?"

The three men exchanged glances. "That ugly thing?" one said to the others.

"Ugly." Elliot dropped his hands. "It's cashmere. It's a forty-eight-hundred-dollar coat. Look at you! You're all wearing your beautiful suits and overcoats of the best materials." He gripped the closest man's tie. "Look at this silk."

The man smacked Elliot's hand away.

"Surely you understand…" Elliot said.

Their expressions of disgust made Elliot stop talking. He looked down, noticing two buttons from his sports coat were missing.

When had that happened? "What? Why are you looking at me like that? This is a very nice coat as well. But the other one's an overcoat." He gestured as though the men wouldn't understand what an overcoat was. "Just tell me where the man lives, please, and I'll get out of your way. I need that coat back."

One of the three men left the group and headed to the reception desk, filling Elliot with relief.

Elliot lifted his arms. "Thank you! Thank you! Someone's finally helpful."

The man whispered to the woman at the reception desk who was pulling on her coat. "I'm outta here," she said. "Call the cops on *Crazy* over there, but I'm at the soup kitchen tonight and I won't disappoint them for anyone. Not even…"

She stopped talking and groaned, looking as though she was giving in to something.

She stalked toward Elliot as she pulled on purple leather gloves. "Sir? Do. You. Need. Help?" She annunciated each word with huge pauses in between, as though he were a child.

Elliot pushed a hand through his hair. "Help? Yes, yes, yes. Thank you, *finally*. Someone asking if I need help. Yes."

She jerked her head at the gentleman near the desk and he started dialing the phone. She nodded. "Help will be here soon."

"Cops? Or the community resource director?" one of the men right in front of Elliot asked.

"*What?*" Elliot screeched. "No, I just need the man's name who had my beautiful coat. He interviewed here today. He got it from someone who stole my coat. For all intents and purposes, *she* stole it. Paid thirty-five dollars at Goodwill. Then gave it away. *Gave it away.*" He grabbed his hair with both hands. "I need it back because it's good luck and… I just need it…" He breathed deep and thought of Libby. "I need to return it to the store. Well, not until next week because I bought it in New York, but my wife's *incensed*. Even though it brings good luck. It does. But she doesn't realize that. And since it's been gone, my whole day's been horrible. Ghastly." Elliot began to pace, recounting the coat's path. "Except for who's wearing it. That person's doing all right. A lady made up with her

KATHLEEN SHOOP

estranged daughter while wearing it. And this man who interviewed here. Did he get the job?" Elliot stopped. "Did he get it?"

The two men grimaced.

"Did he get the job?"

Finally the men nodded. "Yes. Yes."

"Hot damn." Elliot smacked his hands together. "See? Magic."

The man with neat blond hair put a hand up. "He was exceptionally qualified."

"We gave him the job in spite of that coat," the other man said.

Elliot barely processed their words. He gestured at the two men in front of him. "You understand the way the cut of a good coat can lift your spirits and… look at you two." He reached for both men, petting their gray overcoats with long sweeping movements.

Both backed away. "Whoa, partner."

The blond man scowled. "Cops are on their way."

"What? What?" Elliot said.

"We're getting you help," the receptionist said.

Elliot finally realized what they were saying. "I'm not crazy. I just had a rotten day. Besides buying an apartment building for my wife. In her old neighborhood. That part went as planned."

The woman snapped her fingers. "That's where I know you from. Mary Jane's meeting. It was on Facebook and I saw you there all smug and impatient and…"

He smoothed his sports coat. "*Mary Jane's* meeting? That was *my* meeting."

The woman exhaled. "Well, I'm not shocked to hear you say that."

"Three minutes," the man near the reception desk said. The two men and the woman nodded.

Elliot had to get out of there. Surely the police wouldn't bother with him once he explained his frustration, but he didn't want the hassle. Not the way his day had been going.

And so he dashed outside, wheeling down the stairs to the sidewalk, slipping on the ice before catching his balance and diving into his car to get away. *Crazy.* He was *not* the crazy one.

CHAPTER 7

Jonathan Gray left his therapist's office after a long wait and a short session. Though his doctor, Sarah Newcamp, was due at a community event to deliver clothing and food to a shelter, she welcomed his good news about the job and his recommitment to scheduling appointments.

There were plenty of times therapists and "helpful medical personnel" had patronized him, making him sever their treatment, but he didn't get that feeling from Dr. Newcamp. No. Her sincere gladness that he'd returned with a plan to keep this job brightened her face with a real smile, one that crinkled her eyes and everything. And when he explained about the coat and the woman at the bus stop she laughed warmly. "That's an unusual coat you have on, for sure. And I don't know about magic, but…"

"It's that she *gave it to me*. Peeled it right off her back as though it was nothing. That lady talked to me. She didn't look at me as though I were nuts. I don't talk to strangers, you know that, and there I was babbling about the interview, about my troubles. It was the strangest thing that ever happened to me. Those few moments before my interview changed everything. Everything."

A look of concern flashed across Dr. Newcamp's face and she started to say something.

"I know, I know I sound hopped up. I know the hard work is keeping myself steady. But… Something changed in those few moments with that woman."

Dr. Newcamp pointed to the top of the Christmas tree in her office. "Earth angels. Oh, how wonderful to meet one. That's really something special, especially at this time of year."

He flinched at the mention of anything religious.

"I don't believe in God," he said. "Remember?"

She opened the office door for them both to exit. "Well. How about goodness? You believe in that, right?"

He considered it for a moment. "Yes. yes. I do believe in goodness. How could I not after today?"

And so Jonathan and Dr. Newcamp went separate ways. Jonathan strolled back to the bus stop where he'd met the woman who gave him the coat, feeling weightless, full of light, as though a warm luster pulsed in his chest. He wished he could thank the woman who gave him the coat and return it to her.

It was ridiculous to think she'd be at the bus stop, as though their interaction would have had the same impact on her. But he went there anyway. She'd given him the coat as though she gave them away every day. Surely she'd already forgotten him. But still he felt the need to try.

He wiped his bare hand over half the bench, removing a coating of snow, and sat. Couples rambled by, feet crunching on salted walkways, arm-in-arm, packages in hand, teeming with holiday spirit. People always talked about it, but this was the first time in... a decade that he felt moved by any sort of holiday happiness. A miracle.

He let the snow pile up on him. The cars and busses quieted as fresh falling snow got ahead of the salt trucks, insulating the world from the city's normal sounds—people laughing, and blocks away, caroling. He couldn't have imagined that such a simple observation—the noticing of holiday joy—would feel so monumental. Yet it did. The world still held a brightness at its core, even when dark at the edges. He'd always thought it was the opposite, that darkness anchored everything else and that lightness was fleeting. But now he saw radiance everywhere, diamond sparkles lighting on fallen snow, glimmers of starlight in between fat clouds.

He had to find that woman. He looked up and down the street, trying to get a sense of where she might have gone after he boarded the bus. Ridiculous.

He slumped further into the bench. The snow had piled up like he'd never seen. He pushed his hands into the coat pockets and his fingers brushed a piece of paper. He pulled it out.

Goodwill—MJ Berry—137 Starflower Street, East Liberty—$35— Ugly Color-block Coat.

Jonathan knew exactly what he needed to do.

CHAPTER 8

Safely away from Riverhouse Digital before the police arrived, Elliot drove to Mulvaney's Restaurant where he was supposed to meet his family. He entered the bar and realized his phone was missing. Perhaps it had bounced out of his sports-coat pocket when he fled the police. He asked the bartender if there was a phone he could use. When the man brought it to him, Elliot picked up the handset and stared at it.

"Old-fashioned, I know," the bartender said. He mimed how to use it by putting a finger in a hole and drawing it in a circle.

"I know, I know how to dial a phone."

"Second thoughts, then?"

Elliot shrugged then scoffed at the cliché attempt for the bartender to pry into a patron's problems. "No." He stared at the handpiece. "I don't remember anyone's phone number. Not one single person."

"Yeah. I get that," the bartender said taking the phone back. "So a drink, then?"

"Yes." Elliot rubbed his temples. "Ten, maybe. I think ten might do it. Bourbon—Rip Van Winkle—you have that? Straight. Then rum and Coke. And keep those coming like a midday train."

"Wow. Rip Van Winkle? Celebration or funeral?"

Elliot sipped his bourbon. "Feels like both."

The bartender smiled and dried a glass.

Elliot sucked back the bourbon without savoring it as he should. He lifted the rum and Coke toward the bartender. "I just thought of something. I'm supposed to meet my family here for dinner. Libby, my wonderful wife made the reservation. I can have the hostess give me her phone number. Lib must have had to give it when she called."

Elliot sauntered over to the hostess, then showed her his driver's license when she didn't want to give out the number.

"Hello, Lib," he said.

"Elliot." Her tone was cold and crisp as the falling snow.

"You guys almost here? Mulvaney's. I'm waiting and I have a big surprise." He needed to move onto his gift in order to stave off all the terrible things that had happened. "I can't wait to—"

"No."

Elliot drew back, not expecting her to be so snippy during her favorite time of the year. "No what?"

"We're not coming."

"We who? Are you all right?" His mind flew. Was she so angry over the coat that she wouldn't bring the kids to dinner as planned? He was the one who should be fuming after the day he had. No one ever seemed to ask how his day was going.

"No. I'm not all right."

She didn't elaborate which made him wonder whether whatever it was could be so bad that she couldn't mention it in front of the kids. The envelope he'd picked up from the hospital flashed to mind. He hadn't looked inside. It wasn't addressed to him, and being so obsessed with the coat, he'd forgotten about it until that moment. "Does this have something to do with that envelope? Imaging? Like X-rays? Is there something wrong? So it's not the coat you're mad about. Something's wrong. What? What's wrong?"

Silence.

"Lib? Please. Tell me."

"Facebook."

"Facebook?" he parroted.

"If what I saw on Facebook is correct, then I can't even express my disappointment."

"What? The drop-off thing this morning? I moved through there so fast I didn't even notice my coat—"

"Your coat? That damn ugly thing?"

"Well, I want to return it if it makes you this upset."

"I'm upset because of the meeting I saw of you… and MJ Berry."
Oh shit.

"Cat got your greedy tongue?"

That hurt. Elliot rubbed his chest to quell the pain her tone had brought, aside from the words themselves. "Greedy? Me? I'm the one investing in that neighborhood, doing something nice, helping to rebuild. Your old neighborhood. We talked about how it would be nice if someone took an interest in the place—"

"Take an interest in the *people* as well as the building, Elliot. I was talking about people. Not just infrastructure."

She sounded just like Mrs. Berry.

"And I saw how you treated MJ."

"Aww, that angry woman. She ruined my surprise. I bought you the building, Lib. The whole building as a step in the direction of getting your old neighborhood back on its feet, back to how it was when you lived there, when we met. I may have spent most of my childhood half starving and homeless, but you didn't. You loved that house and you said you'd move back there in a heartbeat… but it wasn't even suitable for *dogs*."

"So you repeated that exact thing in a meeting with people who are losing their home? You spoke those words as though I meant them the way you expressed it. I wasn't calling *them* dogs, I was saying that heartless people treat them like that. There's a difference—too subtle for you to notice, apparently."

"Wait, Libby. I didn't know anyone was streaming the closing. I paid a pittance for the building for you. It's part of the surprise tonight for after dinner. And those people can find places to live. You act like that was the only building in America or something."

"Oh. So you have a plan."

"Yes, of course. You know I wouldn't have bought it on a whim."

"So where *are* those people going to live? Where did you plan for them to go?"

Elliot choked. A plan for *them*? He wasn't their keeper. People in real estate deal with tangible things, places, structures. Not people. "How am I supposed to know? Mary Jane Berry is supposed to handle that. Or didn't that part get broadcast on Facebook?"

"They have nowhere to go, Elliot. I heard everything MJ said about their options."

"*MJ?* You say that like you know her."

"I do know her. I grew up with her."

"Well, she's lost her way and apparently can't do what she needs to do for the people who are paying her to represent their interests, let alone for herself."

"You're an asshole, Elliot."

Silence. Libby was always straight with him, but she reserved name-calling for big things, bad things, not for giving her the greatest present ever. To be able to buy a building as though it were a candy bar… wasn't that what he—no, they—had imagined since they met? Wasn't it? They were a team.

"You embarrassed the kids, too."

Elliot went silent. He'd never heard Libby's voice this way, as though it wasn't even hers. The kids felt like this, too?

"Libby?"

"I just… I'm tired of filling in the gaps for you," she said. "For when you're too busy, for when you're too impatient or too important… and… I'm just tired."

Her voice was thin, defeated, but still cutting.

"Libby. This doesn't make sense how angry you are."

Silence.

"Bring the kids and meet me at the apartment building. Please let me show you what I had planned for it. This is for our family, for our children and their future. They won't ever struggle like I did because we're buying real estate. It's not what you think—the building or the sale."

"It. It. It. Didn't you hear anything MJ said about the building? That building is about *people*. I can't even believe what you paid for it. Like you're some sort of slumlord. And after how you grew up."

"The city was going to condemn—"

"No. You didn't hear one thing the committee said at that meeting. And I am so ashamed to have my name associated with this purchase… as though I'm the kind of person who would go along with this scheme. As though you don't know me at all."

"Libby. Please."

"And by the way. We do need that money. It's not like you spent ten dollars without talking it over with me. You just took money right out of your children's mouths."

"What does that mean?"

Click. The connection was severed, cutting Elliot from the bond that had tethered him to Libby for twenty years. Unmoored, instantly lost and ashamed.

He bought another round of drinks, paid, and staggered out of the bar. Just two streets away from the apartment building. He steadied himself by leaning against a tree. Highland Avenue was alive with Christmas greens, lights, laughter as people bumped past him in groups and couples. No one was alone that night. He decided he'd better look in that envelope, so he headed toward the car.

Once inside, he cranked the heat to defrost the windows. He turned the wipers on but they were iced into place. He sighed and stared at the envelope, held it, set it back on the seat, and picked it up again. Libby hadn't said he shouldn't look in it. So he opened it. His eyes flew over the words. He stared at the stubborn ice on the windshield, the way it refused to melt. This couldn't be correct. He reread, slower. The booze must have fogged his brain.

Male—gestation 18 weeks—advanced maternal age—incompetent cervix—high risk pregnancy—bedrest to begin at 20 weeks—weekly sonogram to measure cervix.

He reread the notes, unable to process what he was seeing. Pregnant? Since when? He pushed his hand through his hair. No, no, no. Bedrest? Was that why she was worried about money? She wouldn't be working? That can't be right. He looked again. It was right. Was that what she meant about taking food out of their kids' mouths? A new baby on the way? A high-risk pregnancy? Perhaps she would have to quit work? No insurance. He shook his head. Why didn't she tell him? Eighteen weeks of a secret. And she was mad at him?

The confusion mixed with the booze took him to a place he hadn't been in ages. And as it used to do when he and his father lived in their car, when anxiety had strangled Elliot, he curled to his side, the scent of leather filling his nose. The hum of the car engine, familiar, like a purring cat from his past had returned to lull him into deep sleep.

**

A knocking startled him. Groggy, he squinted at the light, shading his eyes. What the hell? Where was he? Pounding made him pry his dry eyes open. He rubbed them. "Hang on, hang on. I'm moving." The words came as naturally as breath. It wasn't the first time he'd been asked to move along by a policeman. His back seized up and he fumbled with the window button, but it wouldn't work. It was then he realized the car must have run out of gas at some point while he was sleeping.

"Sir, sir. Hands where I can see them."

Elliot shook his head trying to process what was happening. He put his hands on the steering wheel and the officer opened the door, gun pointed.

Elliot's leg was asleep so he wiggled out of the car, shaking his leg, hands up, losing his balance.

"A party night, is it?" the policeman asked.

"No, sir. Not at all."

"A pity party? Or you running a still in that vehicle?"

Confused, Elliot looked over his shoulder at the car. The envelope caught his eye and his mind reeled back through the day's events. "No, sir."

"You driving after drinking?"

Suddenly Elliot realized what the man thought. The car had clearly been running even if it wasn't now, wipers stopped halfway up, with Elliot asleep in the driver's seat. "No. No. I swear." All those drinks. He jerked his head toward Mulvaney's. "I was in there, waiting for my family who didn't show up and I had this envelope with bad news. And well, the whole day started out… But no. I wasn't driving. I swear. I wouldn't do that."

Another man staggered over, but Elliot couldn't see him due to the policeman's bright flashlight in his eyes.

"I been here all evening, Officer Blake," the approaching man said. "And I saw this one stagger out of the pub there. He got into his car and never moved a bit."

Elliot's eyes burned as he listened to this stranger emphatically pleading his case. The man's words were slurred. Not really the best character witness.

The man continued to ramble. "Thought maybe he went dead, but I looked in the window and saw him breathing…"

The cop turned his flashlight on the other man. Elliot rubbed his eyes, finally able to see. He was eager to find out who had come to his defense.

Elliot couldn't have been more shocked. The coat.

This man was wearing his coat. Elliot couldn't speak.

The police officer holstered the gun. "You didn't fall asleep, James? You lying about this? Thinking you get this man to buy you a thank-you drink in a nice warm bar?"

This James guy shook his head. "I'm sober and awake."

"New coat?" the officer asked.

"Oh, yes. I could walk the Arctic ice floes in it. Warm as the devil." He rubbed his hands over the arms of the coat.

The officer did the same. "That's a nice blend."

"Not a blend at all," James said.

"Pure cashmere," Elliot grumbled.

The officer moved the flashlight up and down. "How'd it find you?" he asked.

James pulled it tight. "Some nice man saw me shivering and he just took it right off his back and handed it to me as though it were nothing."

"It's something all right," the policeman said.

"Warm and cozy," James added.

"Expensive as hell," Elliot said to himself, shivering.

The policeman's radio buzzed and a voice requested information. He answered and then grabbed James's shoulder. "I'm inclined to believe you. Your eyes are clear and…" The officer glanced at Elliot then refocused on James. "You can vouch for this drunk?"

"Now hold on with the drunk bit," Elliot said.

The officer ignored him and stepped closer to James. "He never left? Never moved the car an inch?"

James shook his head and put his hand in the air. "Swear on Bibles. The man barely had the energy to breathe. At some point the engine cut off."

Officer Blake reached inside the car and snatched the key fob out of the cup holder near the steering wheel. "You're lucky that James was here to lend you a hand." He shook the keys at Elliot. "Pick these up at the station in the morning."

"But—" Elliot started to protest.

The policeman glowered.

"All right, all right. That's a grand plan. I'll take it." Elliot couldn't believe that his deal-making had devolved from the purchase of property on the cheap to having to accept his very freedom in exchange for car keys.

James gestured toward a bench near a streetlamp. "Join me on my bench, won't you?" he said.

Elliot, still foggy from drinking, stared at this James fellow's coat. His coat. It didn't make sense that this was the man who interviewed at Riverhouse Digital, but what did Elliot know anymore? "Did you interview for a job today?"

James grimaced and smiled a crooked smile. "Interview? What kind of question is that?"

"Then who gave you that coat? It's mine, you know?"

James smiled. "Yours? No. Some fella, happy as a clam, passed it on to me when he was finished with it. Said it like a person was just supposed to keep the coat for so long. Said it's magic. Fella got a job wearing it, some lady made up with her daughter in it."

Elliot sighed.

"Magic." James shook his head. "And he just gave it over to me as though it were nothing. I mean, if it's magic, why's everyone just passing it around like a joint or something?" James put one worn-shoed foot on the opposite knee and spread his arms over the back of the bench, warming the back of Elliot's shoulders. "I'm not complaining, though. I'll have a comfortable sleep tonight in this coat. I feel like a million bucks. Warm as anything."

Elliot shivered, wanting his coat as much for the warmth as the price of it.

No. I wish I could just go home.

The day had frayed him. With his wife's anger, with the… baby! Oh my, he'd forgotten. He cradled his head in his hands, bent over, elbows poking into his thighs. How could she have gone eighteen weeks into a pregnancy and not told him? Elliot rubbed his head, exhausted. He was too tired to demand the coat back, even when it was right there in front of him.

James inched closer. "It'll be all right. It's nearly Christmas Eve. Magic. I can't be the only recipient."

Elliot drew back. Recipient? Seemed a refined word choice for a rough character.

"Nah," James said. "If I'm starting to get lucky then you know for sure there's enough to go around."

Elliot sighed, not wanting James to see his eyes filling, fueled by doubt about his decisions, his life, himself. At least he could keep an eye on his car from the bench while he figured out what to do next. No phone, no car, his family irate with him, pregnant wife keeping secrets. He scoffed out loud at the thought. He couldn't be mad at Libby because he'd kept his own secrets. What had happened to the two of them?

"You don't recognize me."

Elliot looked at James.

"I was trying to give you a chance to remember me so I wouldn't have to embarrass you."

"Remember you?" Elliot studied James for a long moment. The folds in his face, his red, patchy skin… his tatty shoes made it clear this man kept his home in the elements. James, James, James. Did he know a James? "From the meeting?"

"What meeting?" James shrugged.

Elliot shook his head. "*Should* I remember you?"

James blew out his air. "I sort of thought you'd never forget me. I'm wounded at the thought."

Elliot shifted and looked deeply into the man's face, into his eyes, and suddenly the wrinkles and weathered skin fell away. "*James.* Oh my. Oh. *Jimmy.*" Elliot's insides tangled. How long had it been?

Jimmy gripped Elliot's shoulder and shook him a little. "That's right, little man. I gave you my last dollar, my last sandwich, my last—"

Elliot rubbed his face, memories flooding in. "Blanket and hat and scarf and jeans. You gave me the pants right off your body, *Jimmy.*"

James grinned. "Now you got it. And you can call me James. It's good to have a formal name when my entire existence is so *informal* these days."

It didn't make sense. Why on earth would Jimmy, now known as James, be here, sleeping on a bench? "But how? I mean why? I guess I… why're you here?"

"Like *this,* you mean?" James settled back against the bench, arms crossed, his thumbs caressing the cashmere. "I understand your shock. When I think back to when I was a young man with the world on a chain, well, it shocks me too. But you never know. Wife died…" His voice caught. "Died because our daughter died. Drowned." He shook his head. "I still can't talk about it. But you never know. One minute I had everything and the next…" He shook his head. "It's a shock to consider it. I agree."

A slow push of emotion worked through Elliot. He couldn't believe what he was seeing, hearing, feeling. How was it possible that this was the same man? He thought of Mary Jane. He thought of his father, how their lives didn't make sense to him either, how he never bothered to truly understand.

"Remember what you said to me that day, when I gave you those pants?"

Elliot rubbed his temples trying to remember.

James chuckled. "I saw you on Facebook today and figured you forgot."

Elliot choked back a sob. Was there anyone who hadn't seen that video? He squinted. "You're on Facebook?"

"Even homeless folks can use the library. Have you forgotten you spent your entire high school senior year in the Carnegie Oakland branch making sure you made it into college? Surely you remember."

Elliot nodded. Now he did.

"So, I hop the bus, use the computer at the Carnegie in Squirrel Hill, then ride back home, here."

Elliot's throat felt thick. He didn't want to ask, but knew he had to. "This bench is home?"

"Hey, we can't all be lucky enough to live in a car."

Elliot held his breath. Was James serious?

He winked.

A puff of laughter shot out of Elliot. "I'm sorry for laughing, but I can't... believe you just said that."

James laughed too, the two of them falling into each other, gasping for breath after each new round of hilarity struck. *Lucky to live in a car.*

"Woooo." Their laughter died down. "Yes, indeedy. It's all relative, isn't it?" James said. "A person's trouble in life—we all think we understand it and we make judgments and..."

Elliot had never thought of it that way. He hadn't been thinking of anything important lately. He leaned forward resting his head on his fists. "Oh, God."

James patted Elliot's back. "That day, the last time we saw each other and you were headed—"

"To graduation. I remember."

"You said you'd take what I'd done for you and do the same for others. All you needed was some money and you'd do it. You'd do it all."

Elliot sat up and stared at him. "That's what I said?"

James made a face as though he was smelling something bad. "I know. Based on what I saw today, it doesn't sound like something you'd say anymore."

Elliot shook his head. It sure didn't.

James nodded. "It's all right, you know. You forgot who you are. It happens. But I'm pretty sure that person's still in there somewhere." He poked Elliot's chest. "I'm sure you still do a good turn here and there."

Elliot thought of the bag of clothes he'd forgotten to drop at the school, too rushed after digging his own coat out of the wrapped box. His defenses rose again. He did do good things. *I did. I did. I do.* He straightened, his backside numb against the frigid, wood slats of the bench. "I bought that building for a good reason, James. It's Libby, my wife's, old house, and buying it, rebuilding it so productive people can move into it will help the neighborhood catch up to the rest of the development in East Liberty. I'm bridging a gap. I'm a human bridge. So, yes I *do* nice things. See. I do."

James chuckled. "Um hm. I heard your defense on Facebook, Elliot. Already told you that."

Elliot felt James's disagreement that his purchase and plan was a good thing. Elliot felt James asking the same question that Mary Jane Berry had, that Libby had. *What about the people who live there?*

Yet James didn't ask out loud or push Elliot to explain further. He just let the query sit there in Elliot's lap, seeping into his bones where it lay heavy, undeniable.

James smacked his legs. "So. Here we are," he said. "Two fellas faced with sleeping in the park."

"Well, one of us has a great coat."

James looked down at it. "Isn't that the truth? One act of kindness and—"

"James." Elliot grabbed his shoulder. "We don't have to sleep outside. I have an idea."

James looked at him and smiled, raising his eyebrows. "Ideas are good."

"But action," Elliot said. "That's even better."

CHAPTER 9

Elliot and James tramped through the falling snow, arm in arm, talking about how life could change in an instant, how there was opportunity all around, even when there didn't seem to be. The hushed traffic and energy inspired by the joyful season filled Elliot with hope despite how much of his life seemed to have tattered over the course of one day.

They turned the corner onto Starflower Street, stunned at what they saw. The sad Victorian home was surrounded by people holding candles, singing "Hark the Herald Angels Sing."

The old building was lit just as Elliot had imagined it would be when he'd asked his secretary and the handyman to decorate it earlier. He'd forgotten all about it. Wreaths with huge glass balls adorned every window and the front door. Fragrant pine trees in pots lined the walkway from the sidewalk onto the porch. It was as though someone had brought a Christmas painting to life right in the middle of a city street.

All dressed up, lit, swathed in the sound of people singing, Elliot wondered why he'd ever thought to tear the building down.

James put his hands to his head. "Oh, beautiful. The angels do sing tonight, don't they?"

Elliot couldn't speak.

"It's midnight," someone said.

Christmas Eve. Libby's favorite day of the year. And she wasn't there to see this, to see what Elliot had bought her. He had a lot of work to do to make it up to her, to convince her of his plan. Would she listen this time? She was ashamed of Elliot. And for that reason he felt as empty as he had when Christmas brought nothing but a can of cold soup, pulled from the glove box and shared with his father in their 1996 Buick.

Mary Jane Berry stood on the front porch, tapping a microphone that wasn't working. What was she doing? Another lambasting for Elliot Ebberts? He wondered if he should just go back to James's park bench until morning. What were all these people doing there?

James pulled Elliot's sleeve, inching closer to the porch. Perhaps it was time to really listen to what Mary Jane had to say.

It was then Elliot heard his wife's laugh. Something he certainly hadn't heard that day. Was he hallucinating? So drunk he couldn't tell his own wife's laugh from another woman's? Hoping?

The laugh came again. The rolling joy was as lovely and warm as a cashmere coat.

"'Scuse me," he said, weaving through the crowd of carolers and their lit candles. "I have to get through."

There. There she was. She stood in her favorite holiday Target find—the winter white wool coat. Her blonde hair swirled down her back in fat curls. She lifted her arms and draped her mittened hands across Ben and Clementine's shoulders. The sight of the mittens, the knitted ones that Clementine had added buttons to as a Christmas gift five years earlier, filled him with happiness... and apprehension. Libby knew everything he didn't about how the world should work. Maybe she'd had enough of him.

"Libby," Elliot said.

His wife and children turned to him. Their faces morphed from surprised to confused, to sad and then confused again. They inched closer as though they weren't sure it was him.

"Dude," Benji said. "What happened to you?"

Elliot remembered catching his reflection hours before and knowing how disheveled he appeared. He must have looked horrid by then.

He shook his head. "It's been a long day."

Libby's eyes shone with tears. Clementine hugged him, forgiving as always.

"Thanks, Clem." He kissed the top of her tassel-capped head.

"Benji, Clementine—over here!" Elliot turned to see Jeffery beckoning from down the way where someone was selling hot chocolate and coffee. Seeing Jeffery, the kid who'd been trying to wrench open his heart for the Christmas season, shot Elliot with a dose of delight. He stuck his hand in the air. "Jeffery! Hi! Merry Christmas."

Clementine and Benji's mouths dropped.

Jeffery looked over one shoulder then the other and finally smiled.

"Merry Christmas, Jeffery," Elliot shouted again.

Jeffery lifted his candle. "Merry Christmas, Mr. Ebberts."

"Dude," Benji said, backing away. Clem outright laughed as she followed her brother. "It *has* been a long day."

Elliot stepped toward Libby like he was approaching a stray animal. He deserved her anger, but he wanted her affection back oh so much.

She lunged at him and combed her fingers through his hair, straightening his beat-up sports coat. "Listen. I have to tell you something," she said.

The sound of Mary Jane Berry's voice on the now working microphone made them turn toward her.

Elliot thought of the envelope from the hospital. "I know." He took his wife by the elbow.

"You don't know."

"But—"

"Listen." She pulled him closer, one hand at the nape of his neck, sending warm chills swirling through him. She got onto her toes, her lips brushing his ear. Nothing had ever felt so good as her closeness. She whispered, "You gave me the building for Christmas. And I'm giving it back to the people who live there. I'm going to work with MJ on a grant to…"

Elliot froze, his words caught in his throat. He pulled away from her.

She gripped his arms. "I'm doing this. And I know you better than you know yourself. I can't fathom what has made you so…

oblivious to who you are inside, but I know who you are and someday you will…"

"Someday I'll thank you," he said, pulling her into his arms. "No. I'll thank you right now, Libby. I don't know what…"

"Libby Ebberts…" Mary Jane's voice came loud and clear. "Let's get this caboose hooked up to the rest of the train. Let's let these people hear the good news."

Elliot stepped back. Libby took his hand in her old mittened grip. "Both of us," she said. "Come make the announcement with me. We have so many plans for the building and the people who live there."

Elliot took one stride with Libby then stopped. "No."

Disappointment flashed across Libby's face. "You gave me the building, Elliot. You can't—"

He shook his head. "It's not that. You make the announcement, Lib. It's all you. All of this joy." He gestured at the crowd, their bliss palpable. "And I'm so proud that you love me even a little bit. And the baby and… I'm so sorry, so sorry for everything."

She rushed back into his arms and they held each other tighter than imaginable. "We'll figure it all out."

"All right, Casanova." Mary Jane's voice cut into Elliot and Libby's hug. "You can finish your apology in a minute."

Elliot's eyes burned as he heard Mary Jane, thorn in his side for the last four months.

Libby drew a deep breath and released it. "Welcome to the first step in the right direction," Libby said, speaking as though she'd been preparing for this moment her entire life.

James handed Elliot a cup of coffee. "You sure I can live there? There's a room for me in that palace? That's what you meant when you said—"

"There's a room. A job."

"An opportunity," James said.

"Definitely."

"But how? You said there wasn't money, and you're gonna just let me head up maintenance there? Just like that? After twenty years of not seeing me. Plucking me right off a park bench?"

"Yeah. Libby will agree—we'll figure it out. Look at her. It's exactly the right thing to do."

And with that, Elliot remembered who he was, who he'd been before... though he wasn't sure before what, or when he'd gotten so lost that he no longer recognized the goodness inside himself or others.

The revelers stayed deep into Christmas Eve morning, the full moon showering snow-covered roofs in blue moonglow. People dropped to the ground making snow angels, having snowball fights, drinking warm cocoa.

As Elliot watched in awe, Jonathan Gray and Mary Jane approached. Jonathan stuck his hand out. "Elliot Ebberts. I'm Jonathan—second person to wear the coat today."

Elliot considered the man. "Riverhouse Digital." He laughed. It seemed like ages since he'd stormed the lobby looking for the man standing in front of him.

"They called me, you know. My new bosses. Told me some maniac was hunting me down."

Elliot rubbed his forehead. "Oh boy, I can see why they said that. I'm embarrassed. I was out of my mind, out of my body... I can't..."

"It's all right," Jonathan said. He turned toward the house. "It was meant to be. I found Mary Jane's name and address in the coat pocket, then gave the coat to some other guy who was asleep on a bench on my way to see her. And then your wife showed up. All of this. I guess... All of it was meant to be."

"Well then, get a load of this." Elliot whistled and gestured for James. "Is this the guy you gave the coat to?"

Jonathan's eyes lit up. "Yes."

"Well, we have a story for you."

Elliot finished explaining how James and he had come to find each other twice in their lives, explaining that he wanted James to live in the building and handle maintenance when they found the money to do it. Jonathan and Mary Jane exchanged an awkward glance.

Elliot shut his mouth. He was being too bossy. Maybe he was overstepping and should just leave it all up to Libby and these people. They didn't need him interfering. Surely they wouldn't trust him. "I'm sorry. I shouldn't have... but James. He's great with this kind of thing and he needs a place and..."

"Listen," Jonathan said. "Twelve hours ago I didn't know Mary Jane or you or... well. I'm so impressed with where this is all going that I want to invest in Libby's project, in this neighborhood."

Elliot narrowed his gaze, confused.

Jonathan nodded. "I know. Crazy. But... I'll explain everything to you and Libby and Mary Jane after the new year. I think this is what I need. To do something good. To stop just being and actually do something that matters."

Elliot was overcome.

"Mary Jane showed me that," Jonathan said.

"Oh, that coat," Mary Jane said. "Magic."

Jonathan raised his coffee cup. "Goodness. It brought out all the good in everyone who wore it and..."

"Plopped it right down here. For all of us to share," James said. "But I'm keeping it. It stopped in the right place with me, I think." James and Jonathan continued to talk and laugh.

Elliot shifted his feet, uncomfortable with the silence between him and Mary Jane.

Mary Jane pulled something out of her purse. "Merry Christmas." She took Elliot's hand and pushed a wad of something into his palm.

Elliot stared at a handful of material, strings—no, fringe from the coat. "What the—"

Jonathan laughed. "She cut that off before I went to my interview, thought it was too—"

"Fringy for an interview?" Elliot was finally comfortable laughing about the coat.

"Keep it," Mary Jane said. "To remember what it meant to all of us."

How silly that he'd bought that coat. Elliot finally saw it in its full ridiculousness, but now all the defensiveness had dissolved. He smiled at James who wore it with pride. And Elliot wondered what would be happening in his life right then if he hadn't gone into that boutique. "I guess I really did need to buy that coat."

Mary Jane, Jonathan, James and Libby agreed. As they continued to talk about plans and how the whole thing came to be, Elliot stepped away, absorbing it all. He shoved the fringe into his sport-coat pocket, his fingers brushing over the soft cashmere strings. He basked in the merriment as several restaurants on Highland Avenue brought food to the celebration. Owners of businesses shook Libby's hand and thanked her for what she was doing. The tenants hugged her, and Elliot had never been so proud. There was not another thing he'd ever done, on purpose, that made him as proud as all that had happened that day, by accident.

He startled when Benji came up and put his arm around him. "The true meaning of Christmas. Right, Dad?"

"Oh so right, Benji. So very right." Elliot couldn't say more. Overwhelmed with emotion that came with the absurdity, the miracle—that realization that he had to lose his coat to find himself again turned him mute.

And as the crowd dispersed, content and full of the Christmas spirit, the Ebberts family went home, too, full of all that made the season magic, ready to share it all year long.

The Christmas Coat was inspired by a coat that found its way into the carpool drop-off circle at school. That snowy, slushy day, car after car rolled over it and when the author saw the poor thing, and then was present when the man who lost it phoned his wife to ask if he'd left it at home, a Christmas story was born. The real garment that inspired the story was an ordinary suit coat, and the man who lost it was far from being a selfish, lost soul. But in searching for the perfect garment for this story—expensive, color-blocked, fringy and cashmere—one popped up online and now it stars in this tale of bad luck and good people. All characters are completely fictional (brainstormed and created by the author and her two children who developed the plot with her) and any real locations are used in a fictitious way. The carpool drop-off circle is only partially exaggerated. It's a jungle out there. Any parent with a kid currently attending school can attest to that.

Also by Kathleen Shoop

Historical Fiction:
The Donora Story Collection
After the Fog—Book One
The Strongman and the Mermaid—Book Two

The Letter Series
The Last Letter—Book One
The Road Home—Book Two
The Kitchen Mistress—Book Three
The Thief's Heart—Book Four
The River Jewel—A Letter Series Novella

Tiny Historical Stories
Melonhead—One
Johnstown—Two

Romance:
Endless Love Series:
Home Again—Book One
Return to Love—Book Two
Tending Her Heart—Book Three

Women's Fiction:
Love and Other Subjects

Bridal Shop Series
Puff of Silk—Book One

Made in the USA
Monee, IL
24 October 2023

45119758R00049